CHRISTMAS PIPES

CHRISTMAS PIPES

and Other Tales of Christmas Magic

MARY MCKENNA

Cover Art © Daniela Spyropoulou | Dreamstime.com

Cover Design Mary McKenna

<u>Ravensmere Series</u>

Lady of Ravensmere

Lady of the North (forthcoming)

CONTENTS

INTRODUCTION

I love Christmas.

No, seriously, I *love* Christmas. It's my favorite holiday. The Christmas music comes on as soon as Thanksgiving dinner is over, and I watch *A Christmas Carol* two dozen times. (Of course I have a favorite one, but that's off topic at the moment.)

I love it all: the music, the food, the decorations, the traditions… Everything.

But what I love most is the magic that underlies the season: the hope, the joy, and the love.

This book is not about that kind of magic.

Despite my best attempts otherwise, at my heart I'm a fantasy writer. So that other kind of magic wandered in and refused to go away. And to be fair, that kind of magic is completely entwined with Christmas.

So in this collection, I've indulged in my love of magic. Elves and faerie folk, talking toys and reindeer.

Elves appear in two stories. "The Sleigh Crash of '74" tracks the worst disaster in modern North Pole history.

"Rules" deals with the problems of being an elf out in the rest of the world.

In "Angels We Have Heard", a lonely young woman holds on to old traditions.

The most important members of Christmas get their say in "Toy Shop Night", in which many toys express many opinions.

And finally, the faerie folk make their appearance in "Christmas Pipes", my own favorite from this collection, as they always do, with wonder and magic.

But all the stories, no matter what beings appear in them, are about what matters most: love, hope, joy… and the magic of Christmas.

I hope that you enjoy them as much I have enjoyed writing them.

Mary McKenna
Maryland

THE SLEIGH CRASH OF '74

The greatest disaster in a hundred years was unquestionably the sleigh crash of 1974. While the wrapping paper shortage of 2021 had a more global impact, the '74 crash created an unparalleled emergency.

Marcel Pensmith, Archivist

I remember it, of course. Everyone who was there remembers it, they just don't want to talk about it. It was a disaster like we'd never seen before, and we all had to scramble to repair the damage.

We learned from it. We learned never to trust NORAD. And that was the true beginning of ELFNET, which would never have come so far so fast without that impetus. We learned about redundancy systems, which we'd never needed before. The modern world had caught us unprepared, but we didn't stay that way.

I knew more than most, then or now. My beau at the time was in ET - that was Elf Technology then, though the name has changed since - so he was in the thick of it. And I worked then, as I do now, with the reindeer. I've always had a special bond with them, which even the Boss admits. That had put me on the emergency list, though I didn't realize it because I didn't even know we had an emergency list.

We'd never had an emergency. Not outside our own environs, anyway.

Christmas Eve is simultaneously the busiest and the quietest day of the year for us, depending on which department you work in. If you're in Presents or Wrapping, you're probably up all night trying to make sure every last gift is ready. If you're in Reindeer or Sleighs, you're up late the night before and up early that morning. If you're in ET or Weather, you just get up and plan to not sleep until Christmas morning is finally done.

I was in Reindeer, and I'd been up since about four. Vixen was nervous about leaving her youngest calf, who was carrying her first calf - and Lissie was a silly clunch, who managed to work herself into a panic twice a day, so I couldn't blame Vixen - but I needed her to settle for the night's work. Prancer never pulled as well in harness with anyone else, no matter how anyone tried.

I checked the rest of the reindeer then. Dasher and Dancer were always solid. They took pride in being the lead reindeer, but mostly they lacked the imagination for trouble. Prancer, once Vixen was in harness, has no issues, and I reassured Vixen - again - that I would make sure Lissie was fine. (Secretly I thought Vixen was glad to be away from the drama for a day.) Comet and Cupid were patching up their annual quarrel as I got to them - Comet got stressed right before the Big Day, then she'd fight with Cupid, who still hadn't learned to just let the comments go - but both assured me they would be fine. And Donder and Blitzen were ignoring each other, lost in their own thoughts. Donder was the dreamer, head in the clouds and never focused on where he was. Blitzen, on the other hand, was the cool rational thinker as well as being strong; combined, those traits made her the ideal 'wheel reindeer', directly responsible for the sleigh. She also kept Donder focused, a job in and of itself.

I paused by her side. "Any problems?" I asked.

She tossed her head so her bells rang. "No. At least, none that aren't expected. Vixen is behaving little better than her silly calf. And Dasher and Dancer only have one brain between them. Why am I not the lead reindeer?"

"Because, despite everything, Dancer is an excellent lead." I scratched her ear. "He's not intelligent and he has no imagination, but he reads currents better than anyone else, and he dances along the winds. Which you know very well."

The grunting noise she made barely qualified as a response.

"Besides, you're Santa's preferred wheel. What would he do without you?"

Blitzen nuzzled my shoulder affectionately, since I had said what she wanted to hear most.

I supervised fastening their harnesses to the sleigh - the sleigh lead that year was a friend of mine from school and didn't mind me being there - but once that was done, and the harnesses checked one last time, I had no reason to linger. They would start out early - around 10 in the morning NPT - so they could get down to Australia for the start of the Christmas Eve run. Australia would be in barely early evening by the time they got there, and from there until they hit Hawaii at the end, they would race the clock.

Once they were gone, I planned to get a large breakfast - Mrs. C always made cinnamon apples for breakfast today and I could smell them already, despite being in a different building - and then sleep for four or five hours. I'd have to be awake and ready when the reindeer came home, so I had to get my sleep when I could.

My heavy winter comforter, with its not-at-all Christmas colors of mint and lavender, called to me, and I almost bypassed breakfast just to sleep. Although there wouldn't be much later. Christmas Eve lunch wasn't much to speak of. Mrs. C cooked for the Christmas Day breakfast and dinner all day long and couldn't take the time to make lunch for elves with nothing better to do. (Her words, and always said with a smile.)

The dining hall was half-full, with some elves eating before they fell asleep after being up all night and others just getting started with their day. The menu choices were as varied as the elves themselves, depending on which part of their day it was. Some ate breakfast foods, while others ate leftover stew from the night before along with fresh bread and cheese.

I sat down with a biscuit filled with bacon and a bowl of cinnamon apples, along with the inevitable cup of hot chocolate. Porridge was more traditional, and plenty of the elves around me had some. Unquestionably, Mrs. C made the best porridge there was, and the dried lingon- and cranberries made it almost palatable. But I just couldn't. I blamed one of my teachers for that.

Jensen sat down across the table from me with his bowl of porridge. He'd gotten a bowl of apples as well, which he stirred in. I shuddered. It wasn't the main reason we broke up, but it was definitely a contributing factor.

"Shouldn't you be at work?" I asked.

He gave me a look and dug into his porridge. "It's nice to see you too. I'm so glad you found time to spend with me when we've both been so busy."

I didn't miss the sarcasm. "I'm sorry. I've barely slept, I have jittery reindeer and I'm worn out. I *am* glad to see you."

"I shouldn't have jumped on you. Anyway, I'm on the NORAD hookup today, and that won't go online until they take off. I've got," he checked his watch, "exactly twelve minutes if everything stays on schedule."

The NORAD position was a big one. I was impressed and didn't hide it.

For years, NORAD had been telling children how they tracked Santa. Just a story, they thought, to help children believe a little longer. But what we knew was that they *did* track him, they just didn't know what they were seeing. And the contacts were so quick that they mostly never even noticed.

But ET found a way to hack into NORAD's system, and they used that to keep an eye on Santa, just in case. The system, Jensen explained to me, had its flaws, but it was better than no system.

We finished our breakfasts in a comfortable silence, then he kissed me, and we went our separate ways: him to monitor Santa's trip and I to sleep.

I must have been even more tired than I realize because I didn't even change before falling into bed, and once I was snuggled in my comforter, I fell asleep almost instantly.

When I woke to an incessant bell chime that irritated me even in my sleep, the room was dark. Since I hadn't closed my curtains, that meant I'd slept the day away. I shook my head, but the chiming didn't go away, so I finally dragged myself out of bed to find out what in the name of snow and ice was going on.

Somewhere between my room and the kitchen, I realized the chiming was my door bell, only not my entire door bell, which was a pattern of eight chimes. This was only two, repeated over and over, as if someone were pressing the bell repeatedly. I wasn't awake enough to deal with this, whatever this was, but someone clearly wanted me.

Bodie, a friend of Jensen's from ET, leaned on my bell causing it to chime without stop.

"You're going to break that," I said by way of greeting. Not particularly kindly, I admit, but I had been just woken from sleep.

"Oh good, you're here." He straightened up. "Get your coat, do you need any gear and let's go."

I struggled to keep up with him while putting on my coat. He was tall for an elf and my legs just weren't long enough. "Where are we going?"

"Headquarters. There's trouble." He didn't say more, and I, still trying to catch up, didn't have attention to delve into what trouble had happened and why it needed me.

Inside headquarters, he led me directly to a room filled with a computer. Jensen sat in front of a screen, half a dozen other elves clustered around him, apparently trying to decipher what they saw on screen. Another fifteen or twenty elves filled the room, milling nervously and without any purpose or goal.

I still had no idea what was going on, and since no one else did either, I joined them. My friend Sarah, the sleigh lead, grabbed my arm and pulled me to one side of the room so that we could watch what was going on at the computer.

"It's trouble," she said. That I thought was stating the obvious, but I didn't want to hurt her feelings. Especially because it was trouble and who knew what kind. We stood around maybe fifteen or twenty minutes - not long enough to get annoyed but long enough that someone went for hot chocolates and passed them around - when the computer elves finally came to some kind of consensus, and Jensen stood up.

"So, the upshot is this: NORAD lost Santa about forty minutes ago. We don't know where he is."

A babble broke out at that, and someone called out "Like, lost? Or like we can't see him but everything's totally fine?"

"Lost. As far as we can tell, he dropped off their radars

forty minutes ago and hasn't been reacquired. Which means he's grounded somewhere. But we don't know where." Again the babble, which grew louder this time. "We know where he was at the last point of contact, and we know where he should have been. We're putting together some search teams and one rescue unit. We'll move out there, drop the rescue team in a central location, then the search teams will fan out in a pattern until they find Santa. At which point the rescue team will come in, fix the situation and send Santa on his way."

Now I understood why I was here. There were other elves who could take care of the reindeer, but if an emergency had occurred, I was the one with the best chance of improving things. I looked at Sarah, she looked at me and we started pushing through the crowd. I didn't need to hear the rest; I knew what I was doing.

"I'll grab some extra harness with the sleigh supplies," she said in my ear as we got outside.

"Thanks," I replied. I was already cataloging all the things I would need, preparing for any one of several different emergencies. Medical supplies mostly, since the reindeer were (usually) smart enough to avoid the ordinary kinds of trouble.

In the end, the search and rescue teams was quite a bit smaller than Jensen had originally suggested. Sarah and I, for the sleigh and the reindeer, one elderly elf healer who was the only one Santa would allow to treat him, and one ET elf carrying a tracking device. Also, a pair of brothers chosen for their physical strength. We simply didn't have room for more.

Elf magic, useful for hiding and making ourselves invisible, didn't allow us to transport ourselves thousands of miles. If it did, Santa wouldn't need a sled or reindeer.

We needed to use the small sleigh, the one Santa had used when his trips were shorter. Only one reindeer pulled it, and I had selected my own preferred reindeer, one of Blitzen's girls, Flossie.

It was wrong to have favorites among such special creatures as those reindeer, but Flossie could do no wrong in my eyes. She was as clever as Blitzen without her overly pragmatic viewpoint; she and I explored together during the summer months. But she was sensible and steady in trouble, and I could trust her.

The small sleigh with all six of us and the gear we expected to need was quite full and no one had much room, but Flossie had no problems pulling it. And in a few moments, we were airborne.

I love flying with reindeer. I don't get many chances to do it, but they are among the best moments of my life. The wind brushing past your face, because even though reindeer are fast, it doesn't feel fast in the sleigh. The moonlight on a clear night like this lighting the whole world in a silvery glow. The faintest brush of snowflakes landing on you. And to do so on Christmas Eve, in spite of the trouble, the central night of all we are... All the other moments paled beside that.

I didn't forget that we were not out for pleasure though. Even while sparkling snowflakes fell around us blown by errants puffs of wind.

"Santa's last known location was in rural Pennsylvania, about here," the ET elf said, showing us a map. "Assuming something happened other than NORAD just losing him, there's a range of about five miles. When we get close, we'll have to drop very low and sweep the area for any sign."

Flossie shook her head, causing her bells to jingle, to show her assent. And then she took us lower.

Rural barely described the area. Forest would have been better. Nothing but evergreens as far as we could see. Snow covered the ground, perhaps two feet deep, and unbroken in every direction. I shivered; this wasn't as simple as it seemed back in the North Pole. And by now, Santa was hours behind schedule.

Following the ET elf's directions, Flossie flew in a circle, widening it out slowly. After a few minutes os frantic searching, I realized that even though I couldn't see anything, I could just hear the sound of sleigh bells ringing furiously.

I drew Flossie's attention to it, and she flew down towards the sound. And when I saw the mess, I half-wished she hadn't.

The sleigh lay tipped on its side, Santa trying to right it himself. The reindeer, who should have been helping, couldn't because the harnesses were tangled every which way. The furious bell ringing had been Blitzen, who was apparently giving both Donder and Cupid a lecture. From the way the two males held themselves, she might have bitten them to punish them.

The front two pairs simply stood - or tried to. Dasher's harness had twisted far enough that he'd had to go down to his knees to reduce the strain. I'd only seen a harness tangled that badly once before, and it had been a group of sled dogs not used to working together. Nothing that an experienced group should have done.

Presents lay scattered on the snow where Santa's sack had fallen from the sleigh and opened up. The bright colors drew the eye even more against the white and black of the snow and trees.

As soon as Flossie set us down, I ran for the reindeer. The others would have to take care of Santa, but if the reindeer didn't start cooperating, no one would be able to fix the sleigh.

I freed Dasher first, so that he could stand up straight, and he rested his muzzle against my shoulder for a moment and whuffed in my hair, obviously relieved to see someone to help. Dancer ducked his head shame-faced when I unbuckled him - I didn't need anyone to tell me that he'd been at least partly at fault.

Prancer and Vixen walked off together, Vixen nudging Prancer into a more relaxed stance.

Sorting out the back four... Blitzen continued to harangue Cupid and Donder, and I heard enough of her rant to confirm that she had bitten them to stop them from tangling the harnesses further and that she thought them very stupid for having done this in the first place.

I unbuckled each reindeer in turn, sending Comet, Cupid and Donder off to join the others until only Blitzen remained harnessed to the sleigh. And by some miracle or her own ability, her section of harness was still functional.

"All right, Blitzen," I said, taking her head in my hands so she'd have to look at me. You can't look a reindeer head on, their eyes are set too far back to see you if you do that. So I stood where she could focus one eye on me.

"Stupid males! Too stupid to stand still and not tangle the harnesses! They won't do that again!" She stamped her foot. "And Dancer! It was a bird! He threw everyone off for a *bird*! Stupid, stupid!"

She would have gone on if I'd let her, but I didn't have time for that. "Time to get back to work," I said softly, keeping my voice low. I trusted Blitzen not to hurt me, but if she grew any more agitated, she could do a lot of damage by accident.

"You're the wheel reindeer. We have to get the sleigh upright. Can you do it?"

Blitzen looked behind her at the sleigh on its side. Not for nothing was she the wheel. She managed the sleigh, and her job was to keep it steady and pull it out. She eyed the distance and the angles. "Yes. If someone stands on the back runner to hold it in place."

One of the elves stood on the runner and nodded when he was steady.

"All right, Blitzen. Let's pull."

She dug her hooves in and bunched up her shoulders, and inch by inch, the sleigh began to right itself. Reindeers like Blitzen don't come along often, and this was why. By herself, she got the sleigh standing up.

While the others gathered up the stray presents and loaded Santa's bag back into the sleigh, I hitched each reindeer up again, one at a time. Donder would forgive Blitzen her temper in no time, and he had been in the wrong a little, so it was just as well he was her partner. Comet hesitated, but I coaxed him back with a treat.

Blitzen ignored him.

Dancer was last back into position, and he still looked embarrassed.

"Was it a bird?" I asked, as I fastened the last strap.

He nodded once. "A snow goose. They're not even supposed to be here, or awake right now. It blended in until the last moment, and I did miss it."

"Well, I think it's safe to say there shouldn't be any more tonight. Try to keep your eyes open now." I scratched his ear for good measure, then stepped back.

The sleigh was right again, with Santa's bag full of presents in the back and Santa himself sitting in the front holding the reins. He waved to each of us, and with a "On Dasher, on Dancer..." the sleigh took off into the air and was out of sight within seconds.

The rest of us returned home with Flossie flying as fast as she could. I fell back into bed, after informing another Reindeer elf that they were in charge when Santa came home. By the time I woke, it was Christmas morning and Santa was just returning himself.

They'd pushed themselves as hard as they could, and they'd cut it very fine in Hawaii, but Santa had gotten to every house before the sun rose, though he claimed he'd seen pink in the eastern sky at the very end.

By the next year, ELFNET was established, and the ET elves tracked Santa directly. We built extra sleighs and trained up more reindeer, including my Flossie, so that we could be ready to jump in at a moment's notice.

As for me, I broke up with Jensen when he became too involved with ELFNET. I was offered a chance to mind an emergency sleigh, but I preferred to stay with the reindeer. I never forget though to remind Dancer to watch for snow geese though.

One by one, Livia lit the candles around the table. The candles, like the rest of her Christmas Eve dinner, anchored her in a season where she was all alone.

Until her parents death two years ago, Christmas had always been the most biggest holiday of the year. Not the most important, but the one they celebrated the most. And Christmas Eve dinner stood out strongest in all her memories.

She set out each dish in its own place. On her little table, the traditional twelve dishes seemed ridiculous overlarge, even though she'd only made small helpings of each. And she could have filled her plate in the kitchen and brought it out, but somehow that didn't fill the need to have these symbols around her.

Her mother's parents, both born in Slovakia, who had come to the United States as children, always insisted that Christmas Eve dinner be done just as it should be, even to the live carp if they could manage it. She drew the line at fish in her bathtub that she had to kill herself; her fish came from the grocery store.

Other than that, her feast was not so different than theirs. The mushroom soup, according the her great-grandma's recipe. The pagach, which she had made for years, ever since her grandmother's hands had grown too stiff to work the dough properly. The rozky, the filled crescent rolls that were her brother's favorite, which she made even though he wasn't here.

He hadn't meant to hurt her, when he refused to come for Christmas. He and his wife had a new baby, and they lived on the other side of the country. Besides, he had always needed to forget, while she needed to remember.

"They're gone, Livy. Not just Mom and Dad, but Grandma and Grandpa and Babka and Dzedo. You're the only one who still hangs on to it."

So Livia had smiled and said she understood and sent all the presents a new aunt should, along with a box of the homemade Christmas cookies that he and his wife would enjoy.

Some of those cookies, medovnicky and butter cookies and brown cinnamon cookies that no one knew where the recipe had come from, sat on the sideboard, ready for dessert. Those she might take eventually into the living room to watch a Christmas movie later, after dinner.

She paused in setting out the plates to look out the window. Snow had been falling all afternoon, and now completely covered the street. She might have tried to make Midnight Mass otherwise, just to be with people, with a community, but the road crews wouldn't make it on time, and her car would struggle to find grip in that.

One plate at her own place, then another, with only a moment of hesitation, at the place across from her. Two bowls, two glasses, two sets of cutlery. Her table could barely fit it all. But on this night, she couldn't forget, as her Polish grandmother had taught her, to set the extra place for an unexpected guest.

"Always one extra place," Grandma had said, even when other traditions had been forgotten. "To remind us that many have less than us and we should share what we have. But also," and she smiled the laughing smile that set her eyes to dancing, "because you don't know who may come by. Perhaps St. Nicholas or the Christ Child or even Father Frost. And if they come, you should have a seat for them."

No one had ever come, certainly not Father Frost or St. Nicholas. But her grandma's point had been well taken. Though she felt very alone this year, she still had more than many.

A knock on the door as she set down the last dishes startled her out of her reverie. She didn't expect anyone, not on Christmas Eve and certainly not in this snow. Besides, her little house, while not isolated by any means, wasn't on a busy street.

Another knock and she hurried to the door. A man stood there, maybe a little older than her, but his brown eyes, as he met hers when she opened the door, seemed as though they'd seen more than mere years. A line of footprints, already filling with snow, led back to the street behind him, where she assumed he'd left his car.

"Can I help you?" she asked.

"My name is Gabe Joseph. I - I lost my way. Yours was the only light I could see."

Livia sighed. Hers would be the only light; most of the houses were set farther back from the road, if they were even home. Several of her weren't; they were traveling for the holiday.

"You won't get a tow truck tonight, not in this." She stared at him, assessing, trying to justify the decision she'd already made. For a moment, the light flickered and she thought she saw wings behind him, but when the light returned, they were gone.

She shook her head; no one would believe that, not even herself. Still, she trusted him and she didn't know or question why.

"Come in," she said and held the door open for him.

He waited for a moment of his own, probably trying to gauge her the way she'd done him. But then he stepped into the house.

Inside she realized how tall he was, easily six inches above her, though, once he'd taken off his coat, he was built lean. Snowflakes melted and turned to water droplets in short cut hair only a few shades lighter than black.

He glanced around, still not moving from where he stood, while she hung up his coat.

"Your feet will dry faster if you take off those wet shoes," she said, taking refuge in chatter because she didn't understand her own reaction here.

He did so, then followed her into the dining room and the table spread with dishes. "I've interrupted your dinner, and you've got company. I should go."

"Dinner hasn't started." She sat down and gestured for him to take a seat. "And where would you go anyway? Back into the snow?"

"The other plate?"

"For an unexpected guest. And you are as unexpected as they come."

Gabe smiled, the first one she'd seen, and took the seat. "I'm grateful for the room."

She passed a dish over to him and they began dinner.

What followed was certainly the most unexpected Christmas Eve dinner of Livia's life. Gabe was unfailing courteous, though his manners had an old-fashioned quality for someone who couldn't have been more than thirty. By unspoken consent, they stayed away from any very personal topics, they nevertheless found a great deal to talk about.

Livia blushed when Gabe complimented her pagach, calling it the best he'd ever had, which she didn't believe but felt flattered nonetheless.

"I haven't been to Slovakia in a long time," he said. "Too long, really. But you've managed to keep the tradition of it here."

"I've never been," Livia replied. "My babka taught me how to cook it all. Now I just have myself to cook for. Present company excepted."

"Getting stranded is well worth it for food like this." Gabe grinned, then took another bite.

"Where were you going that you got stuck here? My street doesn't go anywhere interesting." Livia had wanted to ask right from the beginning, but hadn't known how to ask. Now he'd given her the opening, she wasn't going to waste it.

"Just finishing a job. The weather wasn't any good for flying so I had to stay on the ground, and I got myself lost. Accidents happens."

"In a snowstorm on Christmas Eve?"

"I work some strange days." The polite finality in his voice ended that line of questioning.

She found that answer incredibly unsatisfactory, but she was polite enough to let it go. And really, it was none of her business. She'd invited him in without asking, she could hardly make an issue of it now.

They talked about books and music and found plenty of similarities. Gabe was more traveled than Livia, so he told her stories of some places he'd been. And by the time she cleared the table and brought out the tray of cookies, she'd begun to think it was the luckiest accident of her life.

Gabe held up one of her carefully iced medovnicky, with

the lace pattern her great-aunt had taught her on her one trip to Slovakia.

"You do have the old touch," he said admiringly. Then he bit into it and closed his eyes. "That is how they are supposed to taste. I may find a way to get stranded here every Christmas Eve if it means I can have these cookies."

Livia smiled. "I can always send you some. I send them to my brother already."

"You didn't say much about your brother." Gabe's eyes stayed on the cookies, but Livia felt her attention to her words.

"There's not much to say. He's living in sunny California - well, sunnier than here anyway - with his wife and their new baby. And he's happy, which is what really matters."

Gabe stayed silent for the length of a heartbeat or three. "I shouldn't ask - it's none of my business - but he didn't want you to be with them?"

"He didn't want to come here." Livia's voice wobbled for a moment. "He said I could come, but they wouldn't do any of the old traditions. And that's fine; they need to make their own traditions, and pick what they want from both families. But this is *my* tradition, and I don't want to give up mine either."

He didn't say anything, just ate another cookie. She'd have to bake another batch if she wanted some for after Christmas, because a batch didn't make many.

She glanced out the window. The snow had stopped falling, and the stars were just peeking out in the sky as the clouds broke up and drifted away. Gabe turned his head to follow her line of sight.

"The snow has stopped. I should go."

"Go?" A surge of emotion rose up in her throat, and she swallowed once. "You won't get anywhere with all this snow."

A faint smile crossed Gabe's face, and he smiled. "I'll

manage." He rose and and headed for the front door, where he slipped back into his shoes and reached for his coat. Livia handed it to him, and once he put it on, he went out onto the front porch.

Livia followed him, wrapping her arms around herself for warmth. And as Gabe stared up at the stars in the clearing sky, she saw that same flicker of light and the shadow of wings that were gone as soon as she looked.

Then he looked back at her, and in his eyes, she read some emotion so complex she couldn't begin to name it. Sorrow and hope, a bittersweet loss and a joy so intense she almost flinched. He bent down to kiss her forehead, and for a moment, she felt the brush of feathers against her skin.

"Be well, Livia," she heard. "Set a place for me next Christmas."

When she opened her eyes, he was gone, as thoroughly as if he had never been. No footprints led away from her door, and the earlier ones had filled in so that her lawn remained pure and unbroken.

She went back inside, half-expecting to see the dirty dishes perfectly clean and unused, as though she had dreamed it all. But no, those still sat beside the sink waiting for her to deal with. Crumbs lay on the table where Gabe had sat. He *had* been there, until he hadn't.

Accidents happen. Unexpected guests arrive. And Livia, by herself again, smiled.

"His door is closed, and the light is off." The soft, barely audible announcement came from Abigail, the oldest doll in the shop and the only one who could see from her place at the topmost shelf up the stairs to the Toymaker's room.

"And the streets are empty. No more customers tonight," the rocking horse in the front window called back.

And one by one, with no customers or Toymaker to see them, the toys began to come awake. Bits of holiday greenery or ribbon shifted as they moved from their places on the shelves, and the ornaments on the Christmas tree trembled as others emerged from under its sheltering branches where they sat, displayed ready for a permanent place under some other tree.

Lydia sat and watched them all for a moment, not ready to move herself. Dark haired and green-eyed, what one customer had called 'very odd eyes', dressed in a day dress of peach taffeta, she was not the prettiest doll in the store, but she did not care about that.

The toy soldiers, who had been carefully arranged in the

window not far from the rocking horse, climbed down, one at a time, from the window ledge to the floor, where they began working on a very complicated series of drills that involved much marching and 'hup-ing'.

They marched, inevitably, right into the teddy bear, whose mohair covering did not cushion him much as he fell and bowled them over. But the toy soldiers seemed not to care. They soon had themselves and the teddy bear righted and went on with their marching.

Some of the dollies, Bessie Belle leading them, had gathered for a tea party, and Lydia intended to join them soon. Abigail never did, finding Bessie Belle's bossing too much, since *she* was the oldest doll. But Bessie Belle never meant any harm, she just couldn't help herself. She liked to have others around her. It was the way she had been made.

The Toymaker had made them all. He had no name but that, at least not to them. He had no family and very few friends, but he made the toys with such love that they could not help but love him back. Each of them, from the wooden rocking horse with his carefully-stitched leather saddle to the lowliest toy soldier, had been made an individual.

No two were alike. They had names and faces that were special, just to them. And somehow, the Toymaker gave them personalities as well. They could only be what they were.

That comforted Lydia, who was sometimes inclined to take these matters too much to heart.

The Christmas decorations, so sparkling and bright, made the little shop seem shabbier than usual. The Toymaker paid little attention to the wooden beams, dark with more years wear than Lydia could count, and the dust that covered them or to the cobwebs that collected in the very corners of the windows.

People did not come to the shop who worried about such details. Or if they came, they did not come back. They came to the shop for the wonderful toys, handmade the way the Toymaker had made them for as long as anyone could remember.

Lydia slid down from her embroidered chair, where she had been placed with a book, careful not to mark her porcelain hands. Tomorrow was Christmas Eve, and she still hoped that the right girl would come and find her.

She stood behind the tea party, her hands clasped behind her back, as Bessie Belle poured out the 'tea' for each of the dollies. Bessie Belle, with her perfectly curled golden hair and big blue eyes, sat in the center of the group, as she always did.

"Will you join us, Lydia?" Bessie Belle asked.

"Not yet," Lydia replied. "I wish to check on the tiger first."

The tiger had only been finished the week before last, and so needed a great deal of checking on sometimes. The toy shop did not give him room to prowl and pounce as he wished, and he hoped often - and loudly - for a small boy who loved adventure to come in and want him. Lydia had not the heart to tell the tiger that with his soft fur, he might be picked by a girl who wished to cuddle him a great deal.

"Oh yes! He was growling fiercely at the toy soldiers, until they drew out of his way. I think he went to the window to sit with the rocking horse." Blanche, another dollie, sat beside Bessie Belle, and though her clothes were farmer-girl styled, and her hair hung in pigtails, she fit there, as Lydia never seemed quite able to do.

"Tell him he may join us for tea, but only if he promises not to growl," added Bessie Belle. "Growling is not polite."

"I don't think the tiger can *not* growl." Lydia left it at that, but she waved farewell and walked to the window.

The toy soldiers cleared her way, but she had to speak to the captain, who wanted to give her an escort.

"You are a fine lady, Lydia, and you should not walk about by yourself. There are some," and he gave the tiger in the window a stare, "who might threaten you."

"I am not afraid of the tiger, Captain," she replied. "What are you drilling tonight?"

"Our pass-and-review was sloppy. But we'll have it perfect before tomorrow." His tone turned slightly wistful, and his eyes held a dream that he would never articulate, a dream that seemed at odds with his stern lead face.

Christmas Eve... Tonight they would all be wistful. The last chance to have a home for Christmas. Otherwise they would sit in the toy shop and wait, hoping for a chance that might not come before next year.

Lydia smiled at him and saluted him, which he returned jauntily, before she scrambled up the window ledge to stand before the tiger.

"Tiger," she said firmly. "Have you been growling at the soldiers again?"

"Yes." And even that was a growl. "But they would not leave me alone. They always go on about straight lines and discipline." He stretched out, his back arching felinely.

She scratched his ears, ignoring his mock swat at her. "Will you behave tonight, tiger? You may join the tea party if you agree not to growl."

He did not answer, but stared out the window. Lydia did not see at first what drew his attention, then her own mood turned to dismay.

"Snow!"

It felt in large, fluffy flakes, like a Currier and Ives painting, just starting to stick to the cobblestone street before their window. Lydia could almost see the snow fairies drifting down on the flakes before darting back up for another ride. But at this rate, the street would be covered tomorrow, and no one would find their way back to the little toy shop in time for Christmas.

Little tears welled up in her eyes, and she blinked them away.

The rocking horse nuzzled her gently. "There, there, lassie. Mind your tears. You'll leave marks on your face, and no one wants a sad dollie."

"I know." She smiled obediently, then buried her face in his soft yarn mane. "But oh, rocking horse, I so wanted to have a home for Christmas. I love the toy shop, but I want a child for my very own!"

"I know, lassie. But better another year in the toy shop than a child who doesn't suit you."

The rocking horse was right, she knew. But Lydia's heart, encased in sawdust though it was, could not help sinking as she watched the snow fall. Would her special girl ever come?

She smiled for the rocking horse, to show him she was well enough, and patted the tiger again, who promised he would not growl if he came to the tea party, but he would not promise not to growl at the toy soldiers.

The toy soldiers promised, as she crossed the room, not to ask the tiger to walk in a straight line.

She rejoined the tea party. Bessie Belle had finished pouring out the tea, though she had saved a cup for Lydia, along with a biscuit. Lydia smiled at her in thanks. Bessie Belle did not seem concerned about the snow or the prospect of not having a home for Christmas, which Lydia found quite strange. But then Bessie Belle was her own self.

The tiger also joined them. He sat beside Lydia on the floor, for he wouldn't fit in a chair, and drank his tea from a bowl borrowed from the dollhouse. The dollhouse people didn't mind; they never said anything as long as their dishes were returned in one piece.

But the tiger tired of the conversation, and as the dollies

did not want to discuss life in a jungle, he soon prowled off to find his adventure elsewhere.

Lydia made her excuses after that, and joined two bunnies and a dog beside the Christmas tree to listen to a story about Santa Claus. The two bunnies climbed into her lap, and the dog sat beside her, resting its head against her until it forgot itself and barked during the exciting parts.

When, in the story, the demons stole the toys that Claus had made, the dog so forgot himself that he growled until the bunnies hid on her other side and would not come out for fear of the dog.

"Now, now, bunnies," Lydia said. "The dog won't hurt you, will you, dog?"

And the dog, very embarrassed, lowered his head and said that he was sorry and he would not hurt them. So one bunny returned to Lydia's lap and the other squeezed in between her and the dog, and every time the dog grew too excited, the bunny would pat his paw until he calmed down.

Eventually the bunny and the dog fell asleep, long before Claus became immortal, their paws wrapped around each other. Lydia petted them both before she and the other bunny left them alone to sleep in the light of the tree.

"Do you think real dogs are as fierce as him?" asked the bunny as they walked. "I want a home, but a dog might be too scary to live with."

Lydia looked down at him. "I don't know. I have never seen a real dog. But I'm sure your child would keep you safe from anything that would hurt you."

"That is true." The bunny walked silently, as bunnies do. "Will the children come, Lydia?"

"The rocking horse says they will, and we will have to trust him." She hugged the bunny, who snuffled her hand in response.

The bunny went back to listen to another story, and Lydia

returned to her chair, though the night wasn't quite over yet. Her own book lay there, a book of fairy tales that she particularly enjoyed, and she knew she could curl up and read it again.

Other toys seemed afflicted by the same feeling. The toy soldiers had ceased their marching and now formed up in their neat rows before the window again. The dollies had cleaned up the tea party and returned the dishes to the dollhouse with thanks.

The tiger had elected not to return to his high shelf, but instead stretched out in the window on the other side from the soldiers and made them nervous by occasionally flexing his claws and growling low in his throat.

The bunny and the dog still dozed under the Christmas tree, but even as Lydia watched, the other bunny woke them carefully, and they took their proper positions under the tree.

Lydia tucked her feet under her and opened her book, losing herself in the fairy tale, until the first pale light of Christmas Eve morning peeked through the window of the toy shop and brought the Toymaker down from his room.

The day passed too quickly, the flow of customers too many for Lydia to keep track of. She had never seen so many people in the small shop. Her chair gave her a perfect vantage point to watch it all.

And over the day, one by one, her friends were found by children and taken away.

A small boy, perhaps six, had greeted the tiger with a growl as fierce as the tiger's own, and Lydia had seen the glint in the tiger's glass eyes as the boy hauled him away. The tiger might have his paws full, she thought.

Bessie Belle was found by a girl with curls as bouncy as her own who never ceased to talk in all the time she was there. They would be great friends, and Bessie Belle would never reveal all the small confidences from her girl.

The toy soldiers went with an older boy, who declared them perfect for his replication of the Battle of Salamanca. The subtle straightening of their shoulders and weapons told her that the soldiers would be quite well situated there.

Even the little bunnies went off with a baby in a pram, snuggled up under her chin quite as if they planned to never leave.

Lydia's little heart felt sad, even though she was very happy for her friends. Every toy should be loved, all the time, but especially at Christmas. As the day turned to dusk, and the Toymaker lit the lamps in the shop, she felt that she would never be loved. And the shop looked so empty with so many of her friends gone. She would be quite alone until the Toymaker made new toys.

One last customer, just as the Toymaker was about the lock the door. A little girl with dark hair that hung down her back in waves and a face like a pixie came in, followed by her father.

"That her, Papa," she said. "That's Lydia."

"How do you know her name is Lydia?" he asked, as the Toymaker took her down from her chair and handed her to the little girl.

"Because that's who she is." The little girl drew Lydia close to her, and Lydia's heart, so sad a few minutes earlier, overflowed with joy. And as they left the shop, she waved a small goodbye over her girl's shoulder to her remaining friends and the Toymaker who had made her.

RULES

Elf magic had rules.

That was what Cara's mother always said. And that her father had left the North Pole because he didn't like all the rules. Except that she insisted that Cara follow the rules too, even though Cara had never been to the North Pole. She'd been born after her father left.

"Elf magic is elf magic," her mother said. "No matter where you are."

Cara was only half-elf. Elves mostly didn't look like what people thought. They weren't tiny people with lots of beards and silly hats. Diminutive, yes. Most elves didn't reach five feet. But most of the time, they were just mistaken for really short people. Like her father.

She didn't know anything about her father, except that he was elf. Her mother refused to say anything about the matter, even slightly, growing tight-lipped whenever the subject came up. Cara didn't actually care much, except that it meant she was tall enough to not look totally out of place in the regular world. She still had to act like an elf.

Her magic had come in when she was seven, and, after that, she had to live by the rules all the time.

The first rule was her mother's rule, not a North Pole rule: that she never use her magic where people could see or find out. That was the only rule she agreed with, because she didn't want to get herself into trouble with someone or something and if people knew there were elves with magic around... well, trouble would come.

Number two was to never use her magic for something selfish. Meaning, something for herself.

"It's very hard," her mother said, more than once, "to use magic for yourself and not have it be selfish. Possible sometimes, but very very difficult. Not something anyone should experiment with."

"Why not?" Cara asked.

Her mother got that tight-lipped look again, just as she did when Cara's father was mentioned. "Bad things happen. Selfishness doesn't work well with magic."

She never would say anything else, and that did aggravate Cara, who wanted to know what kind of 'bad things' they were talking about. Like, would the magic break or rebound on her in some way? Or hurt others? That was important to know. She'd thought her mother would tell her when she was older, but now she was a junior in high school and her mother still wouldn't say.

The final rule was the most important. Her mother always listed rules so that the big important one came last. Elf magic must only be used in the service of Christmas.

SHe'd tried once to help her friend Jenny with her Halloween costume. The costume had been a disaster because Jenny's mom was too busy to get a nice one, so Cara had intended to do just a little bit of magic here and there to fix the really obvious problems. Subtly, so Jenny wouldn't notice. It wasn't selfish, it was for someone else, so that should have been okay. Except that her mother said she couldn't use her magic for Halloween. Only Christmas.

Other beings were in charge of Halloween. And St. Patrick's Day, and Easter and all the other holidays. Elf magic was for Christmas.

As a result of following all the rules, Cara didn't get to use her magic very often.

Her mom said it would have different if she'd grown up at the North Pole. There, elves used their magic a lot, because most of what they did was serving Christmas. They even learned to use it in school, which Cara certainly could not.

She'd asked once, when she was nine or ten, why they didn't live at the North Pole, and that was the day she learned that was the third subject her mother grew tight-lipped about.

All of which combined to make Cara something of a sub-par elf. Sometimes she wondered if she'd be happier as a regular girl, without the magic problems. She'd only have regular people problems and only have to worry about whether she was any good at being human. She thought she did okay at that.

To make matters worse, at Christmas time (well, all the times of the year, really, but especially at Christmas), her fingers itched to *do* magic. Like, this urge to go around doing Christmas-y things and fixing Christmas-y problems.

This year, it started on Monday the 17th, the last week of school before Christmas break. Marjorie Bux Bailey, who always used all three names and somehow managed to not be a snob, broke two reeds for her clarinet trying to tune it before the afternoon Christmas concert. Cara, sitting with the other French horns, discreetly flicked a finger and magic-ed the third one into tune.

Really, that was a favor for everyone, not just Marjorie. If they'd had to listen to her tuning that more than once more, no one would have felt like playing Christmas carols. She was saving the Christmas concert.

Then, on Tuesday, the daycare around the corner that she had to pass to get to school couldn't get their decorations to stay up, and the kindergartners waiting for their bus were practically in tears. That was another quick and discreet fix. A little flick and the decorations stuck. Though looking at the surprised face of the daycare owner, she might have overdone it a little bit.

But that was where 'simple' stopped and 'discreet' became almost impossible.

Wax dropped on half a dozen choir robes - that one had been terrible to fix without anyone catching her.

The special hot lunch for Christmas - turkey, stuffing, gravy and something they called cranberry jelly but really wasn't - made the first lunch period sick, and that had required three different spells to fix: one to make the other kids better, one to fix the lunches and one to keep anyone from noticing what had really happened.

Thursday hardly anyone turned in presents for the angel tree children. She'd had to magic up over a dozen presents, from clothes to toys and get them wrapped. And while that's what elves did and it worked, she was so tired from that one that she could barely stay awake for her trigonometry quiz and scored the lowest score she'd ever seen on her own paper. And that she couldn't fix.

They weren't really her problems, and part of her knew that. But somehow, when presented with a Christmas-y problem, she just couldn't help herself and the magic just... came flowing out of her.

When she staggered home that afternoon, wanting nothing but to lay down and watch a movie, she almost cried to see the piles of cookies sitting around the kitchen counters. Her mother would be bagging and boxing cookies for everyone tonight, from teachers to neighbors to friends. She experimented every year with new varieties as well as doing traditional ones, and Cara could see eight - no, nine - varieties today. Raspberry thumbprints, honey cookies, her special brandy snaps, vanilla kipferl, and spritz were all classic, and Cara swiped a kipferl to tide her over while she looked at the others.

Something that looked like gingerbread but didn't quite smell like it. More cloves and nutmeg and cinnamon, not so much ginger. Some sort of chocolate crinkle cookie with marshmallow-ish frosting. Sugar cookies, those were boring, but they looked pretty with the frosting and sugar on them so that they looked like sparkling snowflakes.

Her mother came in carrying a stack of tins. "I hope you're not eating any of the new ones. I didn't make as many of those."

"Just a kipferl." Cara held up the uneaten half of the almond crescent. "What are these?"

"Those are florentines. I'm not sure if I like them, and don't you dare eat one."

Cara snatched her hand back from the delicate lacy cookie with chocolate on the back. It looked absolutely lovely, but not enough to annoy her mom, who always knew what she was doing without even looking.

"How are you going to pack all those tins?" Cara asked, helping herself to a thumbprint cookie next and leaning on the counter across from where her mom began working.

"Carefully. I don't have much else to do tonight." She began carefully lining each tin with parchment paper to protect the cookies. "I don't expect you to help, you know. You have other things to do."

"Not really. Mostly I'm tired." She considered the cookies and her hand snuck out to one of the chocolate crinkle ones, but before it got there, her mom handed her a spritz cookie instead. "Mom, I've been using my magic a lot lately. This week, I mean."

Mom didn't look up, just made an encouraging sound in her throat. Cara would have been insulted, but she knew that the less her mom *looked* like she was paying attention, the more focus she was actually giving a situation.

"I had to fix the choir robes, and the lunch special, and the angel tree gifts."

"Had to?" Mom asked, finishing packing the first tin.

"Sort of. I mean, I could have left them alone and let things happen. But that felt wrong. And... my magic felt like it wanted to be used. Almost like I didn't need to think about it."

Her mom looked up now and smiled faintly. "Honey, that's part of being an elf. Your dad used to say that he couldn't watch a Christmas go wrong, that he had to set it right, no matter what." She stopped, as if only then remembering that she never talked about him.

"So it's normal?"

"Within bounds, yes. You still can't be seen. But you're old enough to start using your magic wisely. Always for others, and always -"

"In the service of Christmas," Cara finished in a sing-song voice, having heard the phrase roughly once a day for her entire life.

"Oh, go get some rest," her mom said, handing over a napkin of cookies. "You've had a full day and you'll want to be rested for the dance tomorrow."

"You look beautiful," Jenny said, standing in front of Cara just before they went into the dance.

For a moment, they just stood, admiring each other and steeling their courage.

Tonight was the Mistletoe Ball, the event of the Christmas season. Almost as big as prom, and twice as beautiful in Cara's opinion. Their first chance to dress up as young women instead of teenagers.

Jenny stunned in a new dress of deep blue velvet with silver snowflake trim that looked wintery without being icy. Into her dark blonde hair, Cara had woven a ribbon with matching silver snowflakes. Cara wore cream satin with green accents and little gold star pins in her hair. In heels higher than her mom usually let her wear, she looked almost as tall as her friend.

Cara's heart rose into her throat at the thought of walking into the fancy decorated room with just Jenny beside her. It was a ridiculous thought, because she'd gone to school dances before, but this time they were old enough to attend an off-campus dance. Somehow this felt different.

Jenny shared the feeling. Cara could tell by how she kept twisting her bracelet around over and over when she thought no one was watching.

Finally Cara grabbed Jenny's hand and pulled her through the doorway decorated with a garland of evergreen and red ribbons into the main room.

Inside, more garlands draped around the walls, real ones that filled the air with the smell of fir and cedar. Twinkle lights wove through them, giving the room a soft glow. Music played faintly, instrumental Christmas songs, just loud enough to be present without being so loud that it drowned out conversation.

Almost as soon as they entered, someone dragged Jenny away. Not surprising to Cara who knew that Jenny managed to charm everyone and always had more friends than she knew what to do with. Cara valued her friendship more because Jenny chose to be her friend in return.

She just walked around the edge of the room, admiring the decorations and the subtle use of Christmas colors without everything being heavy-handed. She stopped long enough to admire the tree in one corner, with dozens and dozens of presents underneath. Each student would have one, some small token, even those that didn't celebrate Christmas themselves. Cara noticed that someone had gone to the trouble of picking wrapping paper that reflected at least the colors of other winter holidays people celebrated.

She finished her slow circle, stopping to greet other friends as she came to them. But she didn't linger with anyone. A faint itch along her spine kept her moving, looking for something.

Eventually, she found a good vantage point along one wall and leaned back against it, still looking everywhere.

A drop of water landed on her cheek, and she looked up instinctively in time to catch the next drop in her eye. When she blinked it away, she saw the just visible wet patch on the ceiling tile. A glance to the floor told her that the water had been dripping for a little while; a small circle of rug squished when stepped on.

Cara closed her eyes and focused her magic up into the ceiling. A pipe had cracked, leaking water slowly, but the water pressure put that crack under more strain. More water leaked out, soaking the insulation and the ceiling tiles. Soon enough it would grow to where it threatened the dance more than it already did.

No one noticed it but her, and if she could get it fixed fast enough, no one would ever notice. A faint flicker of worry hit her, but her mother's words about using her magic wisely came back to her. This wasn't for her, this was for everyone.

And what could serve Christmas more than saving the Mistletoe Ball?

She laid her hand on the wall, sending magic inside the pipe. The water fought her, wanting, as water does, to go wherever it wanted, to be free. Water's entire force came from its unending desire for freedom, and all the magic in the world couldn't change that. Certainly not one half-grown half elf.

But she had Christmas on her side tonight, and she finally pushed the water away from the crack enough that her magic could slide over it and create a patch.

The patch held, and Cara sagged back against in the wall in relief and fatigue. Fighting the water had taken more strength than she'd anticipated. She'd never tried to fight an element before. Not to mention creating the patch. Getting wax off candle robes was easy in comparison.

When she'd caught her breath, she sent her magic back. The patch was still holding, though she didn't think it would hold forever. Long enough for it to be properly fixed by a plumber. She hoped, anyway.

But the rest of the water, in the insulation, the ceiling tiles, even the rug when she poked it again with her foot? All of that was fine. And she knew she hadn't done it. She didn't have the strength or the energy after fighting the water in the pipe to worry about stray water.

A hand seized hers and tugged her out to the dance floor, where he swung her into a proper dance hold. Damien, one of the senior boys, led her around the dance floor in something resembling a waltz. Damien, who had never looked twice at her in the last two years at the school, now stared down at her.

"Good job with the pipe," he said finally.

Cara started. "What?"

"Fixing the pipe. I didn't catch it fast enough, and by the

time I saw, you seemed to have it well in hand. I did get the rest of the water for you though."

"How did you know?" She had broken the first rule, and her mother was going to be so angry. This was way worse than the pipe. Now she was being punished for being selfish because she didn't want to lose her dance.

He spun her into a turn, and despite her nerves, she moved with him as if they'd done it before. "You aren't the only elf here. I could see you using your magic. I wondered who'd been fixing things all over the school this week."

She stared in shock, but amazingly her mouth kept moving. "You knew? You're an elf? Then why was I the only one making sure the school was all right this week?"

Damien pulled her closer so that no one would overhear them, though she didn't think it likely above all the other chatter. "Yes I knew; yes, I'm an elf - or half-elf, like you - and believe me, I was fixing things too. Did you see the science hallway?"

She hadn't, but she'd heard about it. By the time she'd gotten there, nothing had been left to fix. She'd just assumed a janitor or teacher had taken care of it.

"I could hardly go around asking people, could I?" he asked. "After all, there are *rules*."

Cara laughed despite herself. Yes, elf magic had rules. But somehow, they seemed less onerous knowing that she had company.

CHRISTMAS PIPES

The almost full moon, risen early for a December night, shone down on the freshly falling snow, the silver light causing each snowflake to shine with its own inner radiance. But starkly, everything washed in silver moon and black shadow.

Elanor stood at the door, her body blocking much of the yellow candlelight from disturbing the cold beauty of the scene. Her white dress, overlaid with tulle shot with silver, seemed even more fitting for the night than it had when she had picked it out, though the thin fabric cut in the latest style did little to keep her warm.

Behind her the hall was filled with her family and friends, and guests of all kinds. They expected her to be with them, announcing her engagement to William Morris, and still she stood at the door watching outside.

Her parents never scrupled to make their annual Christmas party the finest around. Food, from little tartlets filled with chicken and cheese to her grandmother's famous great cake at the center of the table, covered the tables, so that all guests could help themselves, and mulled wine and her uncles's eggnog flowed freely.

If she looked back over her shoulder, she would see her family, each doing what suited them best. Her father held court at one table, where his crippled leg kept him in one location, but nothing would stop the flow of stories. Her mother fluttered around, paying attention to each guest to ensure they had a fine time. Her sister, with their father's charm, gathering all the handsomest young men around her like flies to honey, and her little brother plotting how many sweetmeats he could steal before his nurse caught him and hauled him off to bed.

She lacked their gregariousness and charm, though she was lively enough in her own way. Quieter, dreamier, more comfortable in her own company, but with friends enough even if she lacked the bevy of admirers her sister collected.

She always loved every moment of the Christmas party. The afternoon when the young people arrived and headed out to the pond for an afternoon of ice skating, the dinner now with the walls of the hall bursting with guests. Later in the night, they would sing carols and tell stories round the fire until no one could stay awake any longer. Then, when they woke, they would bundle up again for morning service and presents and more skating.

Nothing in all the year compared to this, and she looked forward to it every year. So why this year did she feel so distant and disconnected?

The cold settled in her bones at last and she shivered once, before a heavy shawl was draped over her mostly bare shoulders. Her fiancé William. She knew him by the way his hands lingered one moment than was entirely proper, even though he'd been calling on her for half a year. Tonight her father would announce their engagement and a wedding set for June, and then he could finally be granted those small touches and she could have the privilege of calling him her own.

"Come inside," he said softly. "It's too cold to be standing in the doorway, and your father is waiting for you to make the announcement."

"In a moment." Elanor drew the shawl more tightly around her. "I'm watching the snow."

"You can watch it from inside." His voice sharpened a little, and she turned from watching the snow to face him entirely, never having heard that tone from him before.

He had the grace to blush.

With a sigh - she was unready to give up her quiet contemplation for the hustle and bustle of the full gathering - Elanor took his hand that he could take her back in. But before her feet could leave the threshold, she heard, high up in the air, a pipe, its notes as clear and bright and cold as the snow itself. And it played a line of a tune that sounded familiar, though she couldn't say where she had ever heard it. So she paused, head raised, to listen more for it, for only that single line had reached her..

"Miss Carter? Elanor?" William tugged her hand. "What is it?"

"Did you hear it?"

"I heard the wind in the trees," he said slowly. "Nothing else."

"You didn't hear the music? A pipe so beautiful it could make your heart break if the piper wished it?" Words for it failed her; she couldn't describe the silvery, crystalline notes, nor the tune that etched itself into her being.

"No. Just wind. The only music I heard came from within the house, and there is no piper there."

A second strand of music drifted over the land, through the trees that marked the edge of the park. Different from the first, but no less beautiful. More so, Elanor though. The first bit had held the softness of a long-forgotten memory. This one spoke of the wild dream always out of reach.

"There, you must have heard it that time," she demanded of William, impatient that he should understand.

A third person joined them before he could answer. Elanor's grandmother, the matriarch of the family and the one person obeyed unquestioningly by everyone. Slighter and shorter than Elanor, with hair almost as silver-white as the snow, she wore a lavender gown, decidedly fashionable despite the mourning tones in the color.

She did not look at either of them, looking instead straight out into the snow. "The piper is abroad tonight," she murmured. "And why wouldn't he be?"

"Grandmama?"

Her grandmother looked at her, as if noticing she was there for the first time. "You heard it then," she said. "The pipe's song."

"I - yes." Elanor found her grandmother's blue eyes, normally sharp and clear, unsettlingly soft and dreamy.

"He will call, but you will have to decide if you will listen. Make your choice, but make it in knowledge, not ignorance."

Elanor took her grandmother's hands in her own, trying to find the grandmother she knew in this strange person in front of her. "What are you talking about, Grandmama? Who is the piper?"

Her uncle - she hadn't noticed when he'd joined them - handed her and William each a cup of eggnog, then shut the door firmly. "The piper is from an old story that Mother always liked to tell at Christmas. He plays a silver pipe and lures people out into the snow. Always on Christmas Eve, mind you. Bit gruesome, if you ask me." He took her grandmother by the arm - shutting the door seemed to have changed something, because her eyes were as sharp as ever now - then said, "Your father is looking for you."

Elanor took William's arm and returned to the party, but not without one quick backwards glance. Just before her uncle had shut the door, she had heard one more wild strand of music. One just for her.

Late in the night or early in the morning - Elanor wasn't sure which - she lay awake in her bed, the window slightly cracked, listening as she lay awake. The rest of the house had stilled finally, until she might be the only person awake

The party had lasted til nearly midnight before the guests not staying at the house needed to leave. Even after that, she and her sister and their friends and cousins had sat around the fire, eating nuts the young men cracked and the little pastries that Cook always left for them and telling outrageous stories to make each other laugh - or shiver.

Only a little prompting - mentioning her grandmother's words - had inspired someone to tell the story of the piper more fully than her uncle. According to her friend, the piper was one of the faerie folk, and his piping proved irresistible to anyone who heard it. And though he did not appear often, when he did, young men and women disappeared.

Several people recoiled when she told them what her grandmother had said, and all declared that they would not go out after dark and risk encountering him. Elanor had gone along with their words - and William's arm around her waist - though her mind repeated the bar of music over and over.

The clock had struck two before they had all made their way to their own beds, some so tired they could barely walk and others so awake they'd have stayed up longer except that Christmas morning service waited for no one, and no one was permitted to skip that.

Elanor had only stayed upright long enough to open the window the tiniest amount, just enough that fresh air, cold and filled with the scents of snow and firs, drifted in. But sleep eluded her, and she continued to lay awake.

Eventually she knew she waited for something, and the knowledge of it made the waiting less onerous. She wanted to hear the pipe again, to hear what wandering beckoning tune would come next.

But for a long time, she simply lay there and willed her covers to keep her warm. She lay there so long she had almost decided to close the window and go to sleep when she heard it. This time the music spoke of untrammeled forests and unending pleasures. And before she had quite made up her mind, Elanor threw back her covers and hurried down the stairs.

She had never taken off her party gown, so when she reached the door, she put on her boots and threw a cloak on before she let herself out the little side door into the snowy silver world.

It no longer shimmered as it had. The moon had set hours ago, so no radiance illuminated everything. Instead the shadows filled more spaces, and the ice reflected back the faint light of the stars.

She shivered; the cloak protected her dress, but did not keep her especially warm against the late night cold.

This time, the fifth time she heard the pipe, the sound came from all around her, swirling around like a whirlwind and filling her with the sound of it. Then, as quickly as it had come, it let go of her, the sound trailing off into the trees. Elanor grabbed her skirt in one hand and ran after the music of the pipe, now playing more than a few notes.

She struggled at first - neither her dress nor her boots had been meant for a midnight flight through snow - but when she reached the trees, the snow became a light powder, easier to move in. And there she caught her first glimpse of the piper.

He stood tall, above William's height, and lean as a whippet. Dark hair escaped from under his cap, and his eyes, dark in the shadows, reflected an intensity that unnerved her. The pipe in his hands was pure silver, a pattern of snowflakes lightly etched into the metal.

"Wait!" she called, still running.

The piper waited, though he played a tune that carried her forwards until she stood before him. "Well?" he asked, in a thin voice that scraped harsh across her nerves after the music of the pipe.

"Where are we going?" Elanor asked.

His eyes stared into hers. "Wherever I wish. Tonight I wish to dance, and I would bring you with me. One night of dancing in the Faerie mound, and I will bring you back with the sun."

"One night?" Her fingers itched to take the hand he held out to her.

"Just one. You will shine among us, and you will not wish to return to this mundane world." His voice dropped and smoothed, painting the picture of her at the center of a room, twirling in the piper's arms, everyone watching.

Her hand moved without conscious thought.

Make your choice, but make it in knowledge, not ignorance.

Her grandmother's words echoed in her mind, and she pulled her hand back just before she reached him.

"It cannot be as simple as that. What did you not tell me?"

A flicker of irritation crossed his face. "Nothing. I simply ask for one night in the Faerie mound with you."

His wording finally caught her attention. "One night in the Faerie mound. How many nights in this world?"

A long pause. "Seven years," he said finally, unable to lie in response to such a direct question. "But you will love your time with us. You will not miss it here."

Her sister. Her brother all grown up. William, married to another. She looked down at the ring on her finger, worn tonight for the first time. "No."

"No?" The piper laughed. "I can make you. You won't be able to resist the music if I play."

Elanor clenched her fists in her skirt, but kept her voice calm. "I think I will. The music wouldn't seduce if it could command. You cannot take me against my will."

The piper didn't answer as she walked away, but as she reached the edge of the trees, the music began behind her, and this tune sang of the pleasures possible under the hills, of a life without end or sorrow. Her steps slowed, and Elanor felt the faintest tremor of doubt.

The pipe sang on, the pressure increasing slightly, until Elanor couldn't take another step. But the piper made a fatal mistake. He let the pipe sing his triumph.

She looked back. "No." And she fled back through the snow to the house, ignoring the pins falling from her hair and the dampness creeping up her skirt as the snow collected on it, until she reached the house.

Her grandmother waited for her at the side door. "You didn't go," she said.

"Almost," Elanor said. "Almost."

"But you didn't. Come inside. You should go to bed." And her grandmother ushered her back inside.

Behind them, out over the snow, a pipe sang its lonely song.

Thank you for reading Lady of Ravensmere! I hope that you enjoyed reading it as much as I enjoyed writing it.
I'd love to keep in touch with my readers.

- Visit my website for information about my books and to join my newsletter for the latest news and occasional special gift: https://mary-mckenna.com/ and https://mary-mckenna.com/free-book/.
- Join me on Facebook: https://www.facebook.com/marymckennawriter
- Reviews help other readers find books. I'm thankful for any reviews, positive or negative. Thank you!

ABOUT THE AUTHOR

Mary McKenna trained as a historian and lawyer, but gave it up to be a Navy wife. Now she writes around raising children and moving from coast to coast.

Mary grew up moving regularly until her family settled in Illinois. She attended the University of Notre Dame, where she studied history and fenced on the varsity team. She went to work instead of grad school and later attended law school in Chicago.

She plays the harp and studies Irish, loves college football and bleeds pinstripe during baseball season.

Now she lives in Maryland with her husband and children.

You can read more about her books and sign up for her newsletter at her website: mary-mckenna.com